HANABI

CHAPTER- 1: <u>GOOD MORNING MASTER</u>

<u>2002, TOKYO JAPAN</u>

The cuckoo started its day, singing at 5:30 am sharp. It knows, the master will wake up now, will turn off the button and will sit on the bed for 5 minutes. After that she will get down from bed to start her day. The cuckoo has become a significant part of the master's life. It is the beholder of many episodes which have occurred from time to time from last so many years. The cuckoo loves and respects the promptness and restraint of its master. By the way the master is called **"HANABI"**.

Hanabi is ready for her morning walk. Its 6:00 am sharp. She will walk to the park. By 6:30 she will start her exercise and will walk back home by 7:00 sharp. Then she will cuddle her kitty **NEMO**, make breakfast for both and then she will be ready for her office by 8:30 am sharp. She will cycle to her office and reach by 9:30 am sharp. Yes you are right sharp. Every second, every minute of her life counts.

Hanabi is a young beautiful girl in her thirties. Still without a husband and has no boyfriend. She has been working as an accountant in a small private company from last 4 years in Tokyo. It pays her well. Hanabi is satisfied with whatever she has. She is a girl who has never ever complained about anything in her life. Hanabi never runs out of time but she runs out of emotions sometimes. But she is pragmatic and beneficial at quite some times. She upholds something deep inside. A thick glass wall from which she can see through but she's afraid to break.

CHAPTER-2: <u>MOMMY AND GRANNY ARE THE WORLD</u>

"Hanabi.......Hanabi.........where are you? I can't find you darling. Come out." Granny said with her eyes closed. "PIKA- BOOO GRANNY!!!!" shouted 5 year old Hanabi from behind the persimmon tree. She jumped into her granny's lap and hid her face. She loves the way her granny smells. Sometimes she smells like pancakes, sometimes like bean jam buns, sometimes like those orange roses in the garden, whatever it is; it's very warm and pure.

"Enough. Both of you come in and have your dinner." Sakura said in a straight voice. **Sakura** is Hanabi's mother. She is a tough lady. She speaks less and hardly smiles. Hanabi has always seen her in the same manner. She lives with her mother. Hanabi has never seen her own father. Nobody talks about him in the house.

Every night after dinner Hanabi loves to gaze at the stars sitting at the backyard with her granny. "Granny, why doesn't mommy love me? She never talks to me." Granny said in a soft tone "no my love. Mommy loves you a lot. She can't express her feelings like you and me; she has to work hard for us. She gets tired and that's why she talks less." Hanabi rests her head on her granny's lap in silence. Granny starts telling stories. Her fairy tales and the drones of the beetles created a magical aura all around. Granny broke the silence and said "darling I have something for you." Hanabi's eyes sparkled at once. Granny put a carved wooden box on Hanabi's lap. She opened it with great empathy. There it was the cuckoo clock. "Hanabi darling tomorrow is the first day of your school. This cuckoo will sing for you to wake you up every morning." Granny said with a supple smile. "It is a magical clock. Once you wind it up, it never stops ticking." Hanabi didn't understand much but she was over the moon with the gift.

Few years passed. Hanabi got into the habit of waking up with the cuckoo's sugary voice every day. She was 12 when Sakura was diagnosed with cancer. Sakura died few months later after that. Her demise didn't move Hanabi much, as from childhood she has stayed aloof from her mother. Days turned into weeks, weeks into months and months into years rapidly. The old lady started to shed like the vermillion leaves of the fall, while the young lady started to bloom like the pink cherry blossoms of winter. That was when Hanabi got the job in Tokyo. She insisted granny to move with her; apparently she refused to leave her ancestral home in Kasukabe. Hanabi visited her granny every Friday and returned back on Sunday. Granny bothered a lot for Hanabi these days. She asked her once "Honey, you should bring some friends home along with you or a boyfriend …..May be?" Granny looked at her from the corner of her eyes and waited for the reply. "Granny, the same question again? I told you I don't need anyone. I love you and I have you. That's it." Hanabi replied. Granny opened her mouth to say something but Hanabi stopped her by putting a finger on her granny's lips. Few more moments passed with the sound of the whistling crickets.

CHAPTER- 3: <u>STARS UNDER THE ROOF</u>

Hanabi is sitting on the bed in her small one room apartment from last 4 hours. Today she returned from Kasukabe after attending the funeral of her granny. She is relatively quiet. She is trying to gather and assemble the pieces of her world which has fallen apart recklessly. GRANNY IS GONE.

It's been a week, since Hanabi has not gone out for once. Few handfuls of visitors came.

One night, Hanabi was sitting in the balcony with Nemo on her lap, gazing at the stars. Nemo's warmth reminded her of granny.

Granny's cuddles granny's smell. Everything about her was so transparent, pure, and liquefied. Hanabi wept in solitude. That reminded her about the box she found in her mommy's cupboard when she was searching for some documents on the day of funeral. She ran in and sat on the bed with the box. It was a beautiful wooden box. It was carved very skillfully. Lots of colorful stones were embedded on the top. At the bottom right corner two initials were carved **S.M.**, which means "SAKURA MINAMOTO". Hanabi opened the box enthusiastically. Lots of things were there. She started to take out the things one by one and kept them on the bed. They were mostly junkies. Like few hair pins, 2-3 ribbons, earrings, few business cards, a rusty key, etc. Next on the box were two folders. One was upholding certificates, very old. And the other had some papers; most of them have either turned yellow or torn and worn out. The writing was even not visible properly. Next was a set of uniform. She unfolded the clothes and held in front of her. There was a bright red skirt, white shirt, a red bow and two pairs of red and white striped socks. There was also a badge named SAKURA pinned on the shirt. Hanabi laughed at the thought that what will be the last item in Pandora's Box. Hanabi was least expecting the next and the last item of the box. It was a diary. Chills ran down her spine. She turned the first page with shaky fingers. Lots of origami birds and butterflies were pasted neatly on the front page. Middle of it was written SAKURA MINAMOTO with royal blue ink. She turned the next page. To her surprise first few pages were left blank. Then something was written and then scribbled. Hanabi flipped few pages quickly. On some pages she saw stain marks, they looked like dry tear drops. Some words are smudged.

Her curiosity increased and she turned few more pages. She has reached almost the middle of the diary. Then she saw diary entries which were very neat and organized and properly visible. She thought of reading but cuckoo didn't grant permission. It was 1:42 am. "Tomorrow is Sunday. Best day to explore my mommy's journey with her journal." thought Hanabi.

CHAPTER- 4: <u>THE JOURNAL'S JOURNEY</u>

Hanabi sat near the window with the diary. The morning sun rays falling over the diary made the words look more vibrant. The fresh minty breeze couldn't calm her down. She was impatient to read it. "This diary will take me a little closer to mommy." Hanabi thought. She felt the chills all over her body when she turned the page. Hanabi starts reading.

April 18, 1972, Tuesday

10:45 pm

Hello diary!! How are you? There is nothing much to tell about a boring weekday. Being a waitress sucks sometimes. Usually very few people visit restaurants on weekdays. But ....then something happened. It was around 3:30 pm. It was a lazy, hot April afternoon. No customers were there at this hour. All the staffs were lazing around. I too was sitting near a window overlooking the road outside. Just then I saw a very expensive luxurious car stopped by our restaurant. I ran up to the counter. The door opened, and she entered. She was extremely gorgeous, fair and tall. Every corner of the restaurant sparkled with her glow. She was wearing a royal blue dress, white heels and the white pearl necklace looked magnificent in her small round neck. Her hair was made up in a bun with a white flower hair clip to enhance the beauty. Along with her entered a tall man. He was an average looking man, in his forties and probably her husband. Usually I hate such type of women. They look so delicate. I know she too might have married him for money. I feel like killing them. Basically I don't understand these man- woman relationships. Look at my parents. My dad used to beat up my mom and my helpless miserable mother did nothing. Why do they get married? Yes because some marry for money, some for sex or some just for security. I'm sick of telling my mom that I don't like boys. I'm different. I've a liking for girls. At least we won't have differences. There will be no gender bias, no rivalry, and no sexism. Two girls in love with each other are perfect. We don't need men for anything. Not even to make love. Otherwise, look at these Adams and Eves. There is catastrophe wherever they are together. Well!! I'm tired diary. Let's catch up on some other day.

April 22, 1972, Saturday

11:17pm

Hey!! Did you miss me diary? I missed you too. Today I am so happy. Do you know *Akira*? We started our job together 3 years back. She proposed me today. I didn't say yes yet. But I'm thrilled. My best friend will now become my girlfriend. I haven't told mom anything yet. I don't know how she will react.

After dad's death one year back, mom hardly reacts on anything. And yes, that lady visited again. Today she came with some friends. All were high society, rich bitches. Today I heard her friends calling her Mrs. Yamada. I still don't know her name. But it's true; I cannot deny the fact that even if I hate her, she attracts me a lot. I feel some sort of connection. I love staring at her all the time. Even Akira pinched me today while I was staring at her. Today she was wearing a floral silk frock with a golden hue. She shone like the sun. It's not what you are thinking dear diary. I'm not at all insane. I'm not at all in love with her. I can't love her. Bye for today.

April 30, 1972, Sunday

8:16pm

Her name is **Midori Yamada**. She's now a regular customer of our restaurant and now we share a good affinity. I mean, whenever she visits she calls me for assistance. That's it. What else a waitress can expect from these rich whores? They pay we serve. Good news by the way. Our restaurant is completing 5 golden years on 5th of May. We are organizing a grand party. I have lots of things to do. Don't worry. I'll tell you everything about the party once I come back.

****

****

Hanabi was awestruck. She was sitting motionless and still. "What did I just read? My mommy was a ….? Then how did ………..? This is not a **diary** it's a time machine. It took me so far in time. I totally forgot for a moment where I am." She said to herself. Hanabi laughed and said to Nemo "I am jetlagged and hungry. Come Nemo lets prepare lunch".

After lunch Hanabi and Nemo sat on the bed. She turned the next page.

May 6, 1972, Saturday

10:20 am

Good morning dear diary. We all got a day off today after yesterday's party. Akira asked me to go out for a date. I refused. I hope she's not hurt. Mom asked me to stay with her. Yesterday's party was a gala hit. It was a grand celebration. With food, drinks, music and dance everything was extravagant. Mr. and Mrs. Yamada came and many more guests. Mrs. Yamada looked extraordinary, mesmerizing and unique in the crowd. Today it's really very difficult for me to find words that can portray her beauty. She was wearing a mauve color dinner gown. The diamond necklace enhanced her beauty 10 times. Last night I think I made Akira jealous. That's why after few shots of tequila she walked to me and kissed me so hard that my lips were smarting in pain. She apologized later. She might be thinking, this is the reason I refused to go out with her today. But that's not true. You know that, diary. Isn't it?

May 15, 1972, Monday

12:14am

Dear diary, mom was not well. She had some stomach ailment. Doctor asked to take extra care of her diet. Today she's much better.

But today I came to tell you something which you would never believe it happened. Even I have pinched myself 20 times just to make sure I am not dreaming. Today I went to the market early in the morning. I was busy looking for some fresh fruits and when I was arguing with the shopkeeper for the price, I saw a fairy dressed in white walking towards me, and then she stopped by the flower shop. And my imagination stopped too. She was Midori. Dressed in a pastel white frock she resembled a fairy. She caught me staring. She waved at me. I blushed blue. It was so overwhelming. She walked near me holding a bunch of white lilies. She looked so soft and flimsy. She smiled at me and to my great surprise she asked me to come along with her to her house. I wanted to refuse. But I couldn't. I don't know why. I was getting late for work but still I couldn't refuse.

My jaws dropped when I entered. We passed through a beautiful Zen garden with small wooden bridges and stone lamp shades. It was tranquil. The house was a big and traditional Japanese house. The most surprising part is, her house is just on the next lane from my house just towards the hills. And there were more surprises. She has a baby, only a few months old. A nanny is there to look after her. There is more, Midori is a piano teacher. A grand piano kept in her hall perfectly matched the interior ambience. She is the co-owner of her husband's company too. There was so much positivity and calmness at her home that my state of mind changed immediately. She is not what I thought. I felt so ashamed of myself. She is such a wonderful lady. She is a great artist, a loving mother and an adorable wife and most important, an amazing human being. She changed my perspective. She changed my irrational behavior and of being judgmental all the time. Otherwise why a woman like her would treat me, a waitress, in such an amiable manner? Why would she bring me to her home? She could have treated me like a servant. I always admired her secretly. But from today I respect her a lot.

I told Akira whatever happened today. She looked amused. And she said that it's good she won't have to hear bad words anymore. Her ears can now rest in peace. Hilarious!! Isn't it?

****
****

Hanabi too took a sigh of relief. "Good for my mommy. At least someone was there in her life to crack the hard nut shell, to melt the icebergs inside her head." Hanabi thought. Hanabi took Nemo with her and went out for a stroll after a long home quarantine. Twilight was getting darker on the horizon. The park was almost vacant. Hanabi sat on the bench facing the lake. The swift and soft wind coming from the lake was so soothing that Hanabi immediately made up her mind to rejoin office from tomorrow. After a quarter of minutes later Hanabi got up, she packed Ramen noodles from the food truck for her dinner and all the way home she had only one thought "what next? How far will their friendship go? Where will the journey end?"

Next day in the office Hanabi remained inattentive. She waited whole day for the time when she could go home. As if, Hanabi's heart is left behind at home, somewhere between the pages of the diary.

Finally the most awaited moment came. Hanabi rushed home early today. She freshened up and sat in the balcony with the diary. After few drizzles the breeze was much cooler and the petrichor was splendid. Anything close to soil is so fresh and untainted.

May, 31, 1972, Wednesday

11:23 pm

Diary, today I need to confess something to you. I did a mistake. I know it's uncanny. But it's true. I did it. It has been consecutive three days; I was hovering around Midori's house. Trust me with no wrong intention. I don't know why. After dinner I cycled to her house. Waited there for a while and returned back home. I don't know if I wanted a glimpse of her or just to make sure she's fine while her husband is out of town. I told the same to Akira today. She was furious. She warned me not to do this again. What she said was right. She said that if any of her neighbors saw me sneaking around, they may misunderstand me. And if I get caught they may call the police and I may be punished for being a stalker, which I am not. And the Yamada's are highly regarded people in the community. So, this is my earnest confession. I am never ever doing this again.

June, 11, 1972, Sunday

9:47 pm

June 11 is a very special day for me. Today was my love my Akira's birthday. And I am overjoyed and over excited because the gift I gave her surprised her and made her more than happy. She cried out of joy and hugged me tight. It was my long term investment. A gold bracelet with her initials carved on it. "**A.G**". Akira Gouda. I saw one such bracelet in a movie and from that very day I started saving money to make a similar bracelet for myself. But the day Akira entered my life like a goddess I decided to gift her that bracelet. Today was that day. I still remember, I was going through a very bad phase. Dad died. We were helpless, foodless and moneyless. Dad wasted all the money in drinking. I needed a job badly. I walked into this restaurant to seek a job. That is where I met Akira. She too had joined just a week before me. She made me comfy. She assisted me with the work. She was always there for me.

We connected immediately. And that is when we found out that we are same but different from the league. We understood each other like no one else did. Even our families were alike. But Akira was more unfortunate than me. Her father too was a drunkard and beat up his mother every day. He had an illicit relationship with a married woman. Her father and mother always fought on this. And one fine December night he hit her mother with a rod and fled. Her mother died and her father was never found. Police searched for few months. Then one day they too stopped. Since then Akira lives alone and struggles each day to live a little better. She finds solace in me. Sometimes she gets jealous when I talk about Mrs. Yamada. But I love to see her face turn pink.

June 25, 1972, Sunday

11:10 am

A day so well spent after so many years. Do you know diary where I was last night? How would you know? I was so tired that couldn't talk to you yesterday. We were invited by the Yamada's. Midori herself came up to our restaurant last Tuesday to invite us. By us I hope you know me and Akira. It was their 3rd wedding anniversary. Her husband was in town so they thought of celebrating. Can you believe? We were the only guest. I felt like a celebrity. Akira went to their home for the first time. Her mouth remained wide open most of the time. For the first time we were officially introduced to Mr. Yamada. He was definitely a very gentleman. Babies are not my type of things. Akira on the other hand goes too well with kids and babies. She spent a lot of time cuddling and rocking the baby. Mr. Yamada was a man of very few words so it was me and Midori who did all the talking.

We talked a lot. Many personal stuffs we discussed which were never disclosed to anyone. I talked my heart out. And I also noticed how Akira kept vigil on me with the corner of her eyes and her face turning pink from time to time. Nobody but I understood. The food was lip smacking. And the champagne, we had never tasted before. We had only served. Every food delicacy was prepared by Midori. Even the huge strawberry cake they cut was made by her. With every feather Midori was adding in her cap, I was getting drawn towards her. All the way home me and Akira talked about the generous hospitality and the respect we received from the Yamadas. A night we can never forget.

July 7, 1972, Friday

11:22 pm

Diary I am very scared today. My worst nightmare came true today. But it wasn't entire my fault. It started raining from the afternoon today. The atmosphere was dark and gloomy. There were too many customers today because of the rain outside. When I left for home the rain had stopped but I was too late. I was cycling home. The lanes were unusually quiet today. When I was crossing Midori's house I heard loud cries of the baby. I stopped. I parked the cycle near a bush. But I couldn't move ahead. My watch said it was fifteen minutes past 10. I had bundles of hesitation and dilemmas. I heart said go in and see but my brain said a loud NO. In between all these I realized the baby had stopped crying and the lights were turned off. They might have gone to sleep. A big sigh of relief came out from my mouth and turned towards my cycle. To my biggest horror a man was standing just in front of my nose within a distance of 2 inches only. The man was in his sixties. He was wearing a hat, a trench coat and was holding an umbrella. I could feel his breath over my face. He was the neighbor. Thanks to the almighty. I was able to convince him the reason why I stopped by. I hope he didn't misunderstand me. And I didn't have time to wait. I rushed home with my cycle. Tomorrow morning the first thing which I am going to do is I will narrate the whole incident to Midori before this man reaches to her and makes up any spicy story. I am still shivering and feeling the chills.

****
****
****

The door bell rang and Hanabi jumped to her feet. "Who the hell scared me?" she thought. She passed the diary under her pillow quickly and ran to open the door. Mrs. Ichika was standing at the door with some bowls and food packets in her hand. "Are you done with your dinner?" she asked. Hanabi nodded her head in a no. "Good. I prepared something special. So I thought of sharing with you. Please accept them." She kept the packets on the table and stood smiling like a mannequin. Hanabi bowed with a smile and said "I would love to accept them. Thank you so much Mrs. Ichika." Hanabi finished the foods at one go. It was hot, delicious and home cooked. After granny's demise this was the first time she tasted some home cooked food in granny style.

Hanabi felt sleepy after such a tummy full of dinner. She thought to continue reading tomorrow.

Next evening Hanabi opened the diary, half lying on the bed and Nemo purring around her. But she was astonished to see that lots of pages are left blank. She kept on turning and thought "why so many pages are left blank? What happened after that?" When she reached the end of the journal she saw some entries.

September 29, 1972, Friday

12:23 am

I am writing again just to be sure I am not dead. How could I survive? I shouldn't have. Everything is gone. Still can't believe. Please diary, tell me I am in a bad dream. Once I wake up everything will be fine. Please help me forget everything. Please wipe out the slate clean so that I can write everything new and fresh again.

It was **August 17**, Thursday. It was raining heavily from last few days. But from Tuesday the sun shone bright. Everything all around was wiped clean. Lilies bloomed all over. The blue sky added extra endeavor to make all of us blissful again. The day started like any other day. The restaurant was too crowded that day. The rains have stopped. People were rushing in. I was very busy. Akira left early that day. She had to pick someone from the station. It was around 11:10 pm when I winded up everything to go home. I was cycling a little faster than any other day. The town had already fallen asleep. The surrounding was as quite as grave. Just then when I was crossing Midori's house, a saw someone jump over the fence and run away from the opposite lane. I took a U- turn and went after the person. But it seems the figure vanished in thin air. I hurried back to Midori's house. I slammed open the door and ran inside. Some uncanny feeling surrounded me from all around. I knew Mr.Yamada was out of town. I thought may be some burglar attacked. I rushed inside.

 What I saw was hard to believe. Mr. Yamada lay dead on the sofa. There was blood all over. I started calling Midori like a mad person. Just then I saw Midori coming down slowly from the stairs with one hand pressed hard on the stomach. Blood was oozing out like hell. I ran to hold her. She said in lots of agony "save my baby" and she collapsed on my hand. Tears were gushing out from my eyes like never before. I called ambulance and the cops. I cried for help. Almost all the neighbors came forward for help. Among them was that old man who saw me that day. I was not at all ready for what happened next. That old man rushed towards me and started shouting "this girl killed them. I saw her before. She was roaming around that night. I caught her red handed but she managed to flee. But today I will hand over her to the cops." My pleadings, my cries were of no use. I became the criminal in everyone's eyes standing over there. Nobody was ready to listen anything from my mouth. Cops and ambulance arrived almost together. Mr. and Mrs. Yamada were taken into the ambulance. And I was taken by the cops. Before the ambulance door closed I saw something held tight in Midori's fist. It was a shiny object, like gold or something similar. But just then the ambulance door closed and I was pushed inside the police car.

That night in the lockup will be etched in my mind forever. The cops kept on asking me the same question over and over again that why did I kill them? What was my motive? Where did I hide the murder weapon? And I kept on asking them how is Midori? Is she alive or not? Where is the baby? But none of us answered to each other. After a while they lost hope on me. My eyes were wide opened the rest of the night. With the break of the dawn I heard lots of chaos within them. My mother came to see me. She was crying like a baby. She pleaded to the cops to set me free. She pleaded that her daughter is innocent, she can't kill anyone. I requested her to go home. And I assured her that I will be soon at home with her and I will find the real culprit. A lady constable came near my cell and held a plastic pouch in front of my eyes and asked "is it yours? And tell the truth." I asked her to take it out from the pouch and put it in my palm. She agreed. The moment I saw the thing in my hand, tears rushed out from my eyes. I asked them where they found this. She said Midori was holding this bracelet tightly within her fist. She might have managed to snatch it from the murderer while struggling. I told her that

I know everything about the bracelet more than anyone on this earth. I told her that the bracelet was a gift to my girlfriend by me. I showed them the letters carved on it. I don't know if they believed me or not. Next two days also I spent in the lock up. And in these two days I only thought that why would Akira do such a heinous crime? There is definitely some other person who used that bracelet to put the blame on Akira. But then again I thought who and why would anyone do this? We never had any enemies. We were happy in our small world.

I got all my answers two days later. After two sleepless nights I fell asleep on the third night. I woke up with a knock on my shoulder. That lady constable woke me up and said "you can go home. We have arrested the criminal." I was speechless. I turned my head and saw my mom waiting for me with moist eyes. I asked the constable in a shaky voice "who is the……..? I couldn't finish my sentence. The constable pointed towards the other cell. I asked them if I could go and see. They allowed me. I dragged my feet to the cell. I was getting cold feet. I was skeptical.

 Akira was standing behind the bars. Somebody pulled the earth beneath me. I rushed to her and sobbed loudly. I don't know how many questions I would have asked her but she replied very precisely. She accepted each and everything she did. **She said she did this because she loves me a lot. She was jealous of the growing friendship between me and Midori. She felt left out. The idea of killing Midori plotted in her mind that day when I told her that someone caught me outside Midori's house that night. She stole a knife from our restaurant's kitchen. That night she went to kill Midori thinking that she was alone at** home. But seeing Mr. Yamada at home she got outrageous and killed him first. Midori was upstairs. She saw Akira stabbing her husband. Akira ran up to her and stabbed her once and ran away thinking her scream may alert the neighbors. Midori somehow managed to snatch the bracelet. And that bracelet led her to jail.

****
****
****

The journal fell from Hanabi's hand. She was crying profoundly. "I never imagined it would end up in such a painful manner." she thought. She picked up the journal and turned the page. There was only one page left to read. Nothing has been written after that. She started reading.

September 30, 1972, Saturday

9:29 am

On August 25, I went to the child care home. I took mom with me. I was very scared and traumatized. How will I face her? For now, she's too small but one day when she will grow up. Mom held my hand tight. She smiled and said "don't step back from your responsibility. Midori too would have wanted this. Go ahead. I am with you and I will always be." I picked up the baby slowly. She smelled just like the white lilies. She was so gentle and soft. The same feeling I had when I touched Midori's hand for the first time. I held the small bundle of joy to my chest, firm and close to my heart. And I promised to myself "from today I will try my best to be your mother. I will love you a lot my girl. And from today you will be my daughter, you will be my '**HANABI**'.

We completed the adoption formalities and we brought our Hanabi home. Midori can now rest in peace. I kept my promise.

October 10, 1972, Tuesday

10:30 pm

Today we are meeting for the last time dear diary. You have been a great support for me. You are the only witness of every incident occurred in my life so far. Hanabi is just like Midori. She is full of positive energy. She is a blessing for us. So today I want to write something for Hanabi. If ever she finds this diary I want her to know few important things.

My love Hanabi, first of all we love you a lot. I am writing because I know I am not in a state that can tell you when you grow up. Because we love you and we are selfish. We don't want you to leave us and go away after knowing everything about your mother and father. Please forgive me and your granny for being so self-seeking.

Hanabi, if you find the wooden box just open it. You will find a small key. Turn the box upside down. You will see a hole. Insert the key and turn it right. The lid will open. Slide it sideways. Here I am keeping an envelope. Just open it. Everything is yours my baby.

And don't sit and cry. Move ahead in life. Succeed in your life. This is the only dream all of us has seen for you.

Good Bye diary. Love you Hanabi.

****

****

****

Hanabi sat with her eyes closed for quite some time. Tears rolled out. This wasn't what she was expecting or she has ever expected. She wiped her tears. She opened the lid with that small rusty key. And she got the envelope. She brought it close to her nose. It smelled like granny. Tears came gushing out. Inside that envelope she found a bundle of sheets stapled together and another small envelope. The sheets were still intact after so many years. She read all the sheets. It was the legal statement of the property her mother and father had made. It said that after the death of her mother and father, Hanabi will be the only whole and sole successor of the house and the company. Hanabi kept it aside. Then she opened the other one. There came out a photograph of her mother and father. At the back it was written "With love Midori and Hiroshi Yamada."

Hanabi took the photograph and walked to the mirror. She held the picture towards the mirror and tried to find similarities with her and her parent's face. She smiled. A thought came into her mind when she saw her reflection in the mirror along with her mother and her shadow on the ground "Now I know. A person has only basic two identities. One is the reflection and the other is the shadow. Both will stay with me forever just like Midori and Sakura, my two beautiful and loving mothers."

THE END

9 798721 322150